INSPIRING TRUE STORIES BOOK FOR 10 YEAR OLD BOYS

I AM 10
AND
AMAZING

Inspirational tales About Courage, Self-Confidence and
Friendship

Paula Collins

Contents

Introduction

Hello, intrepid and wonderful boy! Did you know that you are exceptional? You are unique in the entire universe, which means there is no one like you in this vast world. That's truly amazing! Among billions of people, you have a special way of facing life. You are brave, funny, intelligent, and incredible. Never forget that.

In the world, you will find challenges of all sizes. Some may scare you, while others may make you doubt yourself. But remember, we all feel these emotions. Your parents, siblings, grandparents, friends, and even strangers feel the same as you.

Even when you face your fears, remember that you can overcome them and grow. When trying something new or facing difficult situations, you may feel fear at first, but the experiences that scare you the most often turn out to be the most valuable. Learn from your mistakes and find the goodness in everything you do, even when things are harder than you imagined.

In this book, you will find stories of children like you, brave and strong, who face situations similar to yours every day. They also feel fear and worry and sometimes don't win, but they work hard, keep trying, and learn from their mistakes until they achieve their goals.

When they feel discouraged or begin to doubt themselves, these children find that unique light within them that helps them keep going, even when they think about giving up. In each story, these children discover self-confidence, hope, and courage that allow them to live incredible experiences in every situation, leading them to reach their dreams.

Now is the time to light up your corner of the world. Share your light with others, free yourself from fear, and learn life's lessons. Believe in yourself, and you can accomplish anything.

You are an amazing and unique boy!

Embracing New Adventures

Have you ever imagined how many kilometers the world is? Billions? How do you think they live? Do you think they are like you or do their own thing? This story shows how every culture is different and has its own ways of living.

Since Alex had arrived in that new country after traveling many hours on a plane where he felt like he had circled the planet eight times, they finally landed.

He had already seen people everywhere who spoke a little differently than him, who had a different way of being—the clothes, their faces, the way they even walked. He knew he was not at home and that it was a different culture.

Already at his cousins' house, where he had gone to spend some time, at his uncle's house, he had dinner in front of him; it was a plate with many vegetables on top, almost covering his head. Alex looked at them with fear.

His cousin was next to him and looked at him strangely.

"What is this, Charlie?" He asked his cousin.

"Food."

"Yes, but I haven't seen it. What is that yellow stuff?" He asked again.

"They are all vegetables, and if you try them, you will like them. We eat them a lot here."

Charlie couldn't stop looking at him with amusement.

"Since I came to this place, everything has been so... strange," Alex said.

"No, it's not weird. I think if I went to your country, the same thing would happen to me. It's called culture; we are all different." His cousin told him very kindly.

Alex finally dared to take a piece of food and taste it. He did it with the one that seemed the strangest to him, expecting to find a bitter taste, but he opened his eyes and said,

"This tastes very good."

"Everything is delicious. Give yourself a chance to enjoy it."

He continued tasting other foods—the meat, the other vegetables, some he knew—and he felt that each one had a new flavor, and although one or another he didn't like so much, he still ate it; his mother had taught him not to leave anything on the plate.

His aunt, along with his cousin, were the ones who had gone to pick him up at the airport. His uncle had

not gone because he was working, and they did not know each other, so there was a lot of expectation for how that first meeting would be. Alex went by asking what he was like, if he seemed in a good mood, and if he was affectionate.

His cousin, who was fond of making jokes, told him that he was sullen, that he would get angry for nothing, and then told him the truth—that he was not, that he was loving and very playful.

As Alex had so many things on his mind, anything could happen, and he was afraid.

As time went by, he played with his cousin and talked to his parents by video call. In his country, it was already night, and where he was at that moment, there was still a very bright sun. That also seemed curious to him, as he had always heard that it did not get dark at the same time all over the world due to the movement of the planet, but living it was a totally different experience.

Finally, his uncle arrived, walked through the door, and stood looking at him.

"This is a lovely boy," said the uncle, opening his arms and pulling him in to greet him.

His uncle was a thin man dressed in a suit who had a big mustache covering his upper lip.

"Hello, uncle," he said as he ran to greet him.

He picked him up and pressed him against his chest as he planted a kiss on his cheek.

Although he spoke Alex's language, he had a strange accent that he couldn't quite put his finger on. He found the way he spoke funny but said nothing.

Long before coming on this trip, Alex had seen that his aunt wore different clothes from his own. He noticed several pictures, and he especially liked the one with the purple and pink suit. It was beautiful and colorful. He had never seen anything like it, and he asked his mother why they dressed like that.

"It's the way they dress in their country. Don't you like it?" his mother said.

"Yes, I like these dresses, although I don't like my uncle's shirt. I think it's too flashy. Dad wears shirts with one color."

The mother laughed and told him they were a bit showy, but that's how they wore them there.

Now, in his uncle's and cousin's country, he stood before his aunt, who had a beautiful suit with gold lace and other flashy shades all over her garment, and his uncle, who, although dressed smartly, had a flashy shirt underneath.

"What do you like to play in your country?" asked his uncle.

"I play soccer a lot. I have some friends in my area with whom we have a lot of fun. I love it." He said.

"I see. Do you want to play?" asked his uncle.

Alex agreed immediately.

The three of them went out to the backyard of the house, and from somewhere they took out a big ball, like the professionals, and began to play without any rules of the sport, simply playing to take it away from each other and scoring in a door that served as an archery.

They had a lot of fun with their games. They spent at least an hour until the uncle, already sweaty and tired, sat down and asked for a break.

"Go on, children; this old man can't go on any longer," he said.

The two children laughed and continued playing; this time, one shot, and the other tried to catch the ball.

When they were both tired too, they went into the house. The cousin's mother appeared with some brightly colored drinks that she said were from local fruit. For Alex, again, it was a challenge. Still, he remembered that his mother had told him that he had to try new things in that country and that whatever they gave him, even though he didn't know it, would be a unique experience. He couldn't refuse it without trying it first.

He held his breath, took the first sip, and tasted it. He was surprised. It was sweet; he could not describe it, but it was like a mixture of watermelon for its refreshing, banana for its creaminess, and peach for its consistency. But it was more; it was as if he had mixed many fruits. He asked his aunt, but she said no, it was only one fruit, and that she would show it to him later.

"We have a present for you," said his uncle.

He motioned to his cousin's mother, and she went off into one of the rooms and soon after returned with a box that was wrapped in wrapping paper. If Alex had seen flashy things so far, this was the most attractive

of all, very colorful with colors that, if you put them against the sun, would illuminate a whole street.

He began to uncover the gift, which had a red ribbon with a beautiful bow on top. It was light, and he could not imagine what it could be. He unwrapped it while his uncle, aunt, and cousin watched expectantly for his reaction.

When he uncovered it, he found something that lit up his face. It was a finely folded piece of cloth. He touched it. It was very soft. It could almost slide through his fingers.

He took it out. It was a traditional outfit with golden lace at the corners of the sleeves and neck. He knew immediately that it would fit him perfectly, as if he had been measured.

"Your mother told us that you liked some of my outfits," said his aunt.

Alex nodded.

"Our tailor-made one with the measurements your mother sent."

Alex remembered that weeks ago his mother had been going through a lot of his clothes; he knew she

was preparing the surprise at that moment, so he made a mental note that he would congratulate her.

He spent the vacation season learning new things, being open to enjoying every experience, and dressing as if he were just another local. He knew that giving himself the opportunity to learn about other cultures and respecting them was the best way to nurture his experiences.

If you dare to enjoy each new culture, venture into worlds you have not seen before, respecting what each one has. You will enter a universe where you will come out more prepared and know that the world is different and rich in customs.

Courageous like a Bear

There are situations in life that force us to be brave. Whether it's going to the doctor or riding a bike, being brave means you stand up for yourself and aren't afraid of anything. In this story, you will see Andy's bravery put to the test. True bravery lies within us; all it takes is a little push, and you'll be just like Andy when he went camping.

Today is an exciting day; Andy and his class are going on a field trip! Andy has been excited for some time to go camping, and now the day has finally arrived. He packed his bag, said goodbye to his mom and dad, got in the bus car, and sat down next to his friend Charlie to head to school.

"Are you ready for camp?" Andy asks.

"Yes, I am; why are you so excited?" Charlie asked.

There were many things Andy was excited about, like walking in the woods, roasting marshmallows, telling camp stories, or scavenger hunts! The list was long, but overall, Andy was very excited to spend a few days outdoors, just like when he went camping with his dad.

Andy looked out the window as they arrived at school; upon arrival, he went to his classroom and stood at attention to answer when his roll was called.

"Here!" he said when he heard his name. The teacher crossed him off the list, and so did the rest of the class as they waited for the bus to take them on the field trip. He could hardly contain his excitement!

When the bus arrived, Andy and his classmates excitedly loaded their bags onto the bus.

On the trip, Andy sat next to Charlie, chatting and laughing with joy.

On the way, they played spy games and riddles to pass the time.

After a while, Andy exclaimed, "I see the camp!" pointing out the window.

All the companions were happy when they reached the camp.

There were many trees and plants everywhere. Andy and his class would soon learn a lot from them.

"I can hardly wait; what will we go do first?" wondered Charlie.

All the children got off the bus and were greeted by the camp guide, Marco.

Marco would be the one in charge of assigning bunk beds and would take them on adventures in the woods.

"I hope everyone is as excited as I am," Marco said.

He divided the class into boys and girls and allowed them to settle into their bunks. Andy sat on his bed and began writing in his journal about this adventure

before Marco pointed out to them that they would soon be walking down a trail.

"I can't wait!" said Andy, and he got ready to line up to leave. Andy received a list of all the items required to complete the treasure hunt and was confident that he would be able to complete the tasks successfully.

Marco led the children down the trail, and Andy listened to all the sounds of nature, like birds chirping, owls hooting, and the wind rustling in the bushes. He was already having so much fun and couldn't wait to see what was next.

"I found an acorn," Andy said, stuffing it into his bag. He found many of his items, but as the class continued down the trail, Andy stopped when he saw another path he wanted to go down.

He knew he shouldn't go too far, but he was very tempted to try something new.

"I don't think they'll mind," Andy thought and broke away from his group, finding more items like rocks, pinecones, and shells.

"I'm almost done," Andy thought, crossing off his list of what he was getting. He continued to wander down the path with curiosity.

When Andy had already advanced along the new path, he realized that he might have made a mistake. He couldn't remember how to get back on the right path. He was so far from his classroom that he couldn't ask for help.

"I have the compass that my dad gave me to find my way," Andy said, reaching into his pocket to pull it out.

With the help of the compass, Andy kept walking and went deeper into the forest, looking for the way back. The sun was already setting, and Andy needed to get back to his class, but suddenly, he heard a rustling sound coming from behind a tree.

He wanted to investigate, so he approached the mysterious noise when suddenly, from behind the bushes, a bear appeared!

Andy froze in fear; the bear approached and began to sniff him. He had never encountered a bear before and didn't know what to do. Andy stood still while the bear looked at him curiously. He tried to scream for help, but no one heard him, and he only succeeded in making the bear more interested in him.

"I can't be bear food!" Andy thought to himself, and at that moment, a brilliant idea occurred to him.

He remembered that he was carrying some candy in his pocket that his mom had given him when she said goodbye to him, wishing him good luck.

He took the candies and slowly showed them to the bear to sniff; when he managed to get his attention, he threw them as far as he could, making the bear go after them. Andy ran as fast as he could to get out of the bear's sight and managed to escape. Once he felt safe, he tried to find his way back to where his companions were supposed to be.

"Where are they?" said Andy, looking in all directions until he heard his friends in the distance and ran to join them.

The classmates were relieved to see Andy coming; they were very worried because they could not manage to find him. They surrounded him to greet him and ask him where he had been.

"I'm so glad to have found you; I thought I was lost forever!" Andy said.

"I ran into a big bear, and I thought he was going to eat me," he continued, "until I was able to distract him by throwing some candy I had in my pocket, and I managed to run away."

"Andy, that's why we shouldn't stray from the path, this one is safe, but in the forest, some bears have been spotted that I'm sure you wouldn't want to encounter; it could be dangerous. You could have been badly hurt," said Marco.

Listening to Andy's story, his classmates applauded him in admiration, and Marco was very proud of him for having been so brave.

"What you did was very smart, you kept your cool, and with your bravery, you managed to get to safety," said Marco.

When they returned to camp, they lit the campfire, told stories, and roasted marshmallows. Andy and Charlie sat together in the warmth of the fire.

"I'm so glad you're okay, Andy," Charlie hugged him.

"Me too, it was really scary, and I almost didn't know what to do," Andy put his marshmallow on the fire.

"Attention, everyone. We have a very special award to present at this time," Marco said.

"We will present this award to someone for fearless and smart."

"Andy, today you are being awarded for your bravery. You faced a bear and were able to protect yourself, and that takes a lot of courage to do that," Marco presented Andy with the bravery medal as an award.

"Wow, I can't believe it. I've never won a bravery award before. I can't wait to show it to my parents." Andy said, hugging the award tightly. "This means so much to me!"

At the end of the night, everyone went back to their bunks, and Andy wrote everything down in his journal and told the story of how he managed to trick the bear. His classmates were amazed and admired Andy for his bravery. Andy was as courageous as a bear.

Being brave is about being fearless and taking on challenges, just like Andy. He was scared and lost and fought off a bear, all because he didn't back down and showed true bravery.

We can all show courage every day by trying new things and never backing down, no matter what anyone says or how we feel.

When you find the roar inside you, you will be strong and not afraid of anything.

The Reckless Skateboarder

Do your parents ask you not to do things, and you feel it is unfair? Do they warn you of the dangers you may encounter along the way? This is a story that shows how disobeying the rules can have serious consequences.

Jack loved skateboards; when it was his birthday, he asked months in advance for that to be his present. He was begging to receive it and to be able to start playing with his friend Sam around the blocks from home.

He was lucky enough to receive it and tell his neighbor to go and play. He seemed to have been born for it; he skated perfectly, did not fall, and moved smoothly from one side to the other, breaking without any problem.

Soon he was already doing some tricks and lifting the front of the skateboard off the ground.

He had a few falls, but they were not serious.

Jack's father was loving to please him in whatever he asked, but he also had a temper and always asked him how to do things or to protect himself so that nothing would happen to him. If he forbade him to do something, he had to comply and beware of breaking that rule because there would be consequences with punishments lasting weeks.

Jack didn't like it when his father gave him that look. He was the one who demanded order, that the room was nice, that he bathed and brushed on time, that

he did his homework on time, and all that he didn't like sometimes. Now he looked at him sternly, as if waiting for a response from him for doing something he didn't know if it was wrong or not.

"I think I told you that you could play in this whole area, along the front of the dead-end street, not go out on the main road, let alone look out over the slope." he said.

"But Sam and I have barely looked out. Besides, we are careful not to go down there."

"But you were so close, I saw you, inches away from the slope, one carelessness, and you would go down that slope, and who knows what would happen? You would fall, break a bone, or worse, get hit by a car below."

"But we won't do it."

"You have to abide by that rule, or I'm confiscating your skateboard until further notice."

The father entered the house after giving the warning, and Jack saw Sam.

"Dad forbids me to do everything. He always controls me. I can't stand a lot of things sometimes."

The father seemed to hear what Jack said because he came back.

Sam, to avoid witnessing more trouble, began to skate, went around the hill and did a trick, and came back with speed.

"You see, dad, Sam does all that without a problem. He doesn't even fall."

"He's not my son. You are. When I ask you not to do it, I know why I'm saying it; it's not a whim. I'm protecting you. I had put up with buying you the skateboard because I didn't want anything to happen to you, and your friend lives in a flat area with more space. We have that slope there that I'm afraid might cause something to happen to you."

The father asked him to get off the skateboard and took him inside, grounded for three weeks. It was a harsh measure, but it was his way of educating and telling him how to do things.

After this punishment, he was able to go out with Sam; his father was out with friends; and his mother was taking a nap. It was the perfect time to have fun with the skateboard.

He did more tricks than ever, jumped over mounds, moved around, jumped over some benches, and managed it quite fluently. Jack felt free to do some flips that would surely have made his father jump to confiscate the thing again.

"What if we went down the slope?" said Sam mischievously.

"But my dad..."

"He's not here; come on."

Jack knew that facing that danger was one thing, but facing it was quite another, so he thought about it for a moment and finally decided to accept it and take the plunge.

The first one to do it was Sam, who stood on the skateboard and, with one foot, propelled himself. When he reached the slope, he put himself on top, in a position to keep his balance, and descended at great speed. When he approached the part where the cars passed, he turned easily and stopped on a small ramp; from there, he pointed with his finger that everything was fine.

Jack thought about everything again. His father was gone, his mother was asleep, and it was now or never

that he could face that temptation that always called him. Surely nothing would happen if he was a great skater.

He started down the hill, the skateboard vibrated under his feet, he picked up more and more speed, and the air hit his face. It felt great—fear, adrenaline, danger, breaking the rules.

Sam seemed to scream but didn't hear. He tried to make the turn but didn't, and he kept going straight ahead. Tires screeched, he lost his balance, and Jack ran over the car and fell on the hood. He was looking straight at the passenger seat, and there, his father looked scared.

Jack's father got out of the car, rushed him off the hood, and put him on the sidewalk to check that he was okay. He was extremely scared. He began to check his back, his sides, his legs, and his neck and asked him to move his limbs to confirm that he was okay.

When he saw that he was fine, beyond the scare and the fact that he had fallen like a sack on the hood, nothing had happened to him. He carried him in his arms to the house and pushed him as he walked up the hill, but not once did he complain.

Once at the door, he stood Jack up and firmly took him by the hand. His father had never reprimanded him with violence; he knew of children who were spanked, and he imagined that having broken this rule meant that for the first time, they would learn it. His father's silence and the way he looked at him and moved made him think so.

His father, who had his eyes wide open and was far from starting to scold him, told him in a voice broken with tears:

"Son, you could have died. Do you realize how close you came to suffering a serious accident?"

Then he hugged him and held him for a long time like that, while he seemed to be thankful that it hadn't happened.

The skateboard was confiscated until further notice, until he showed that he could be trusted. Although Jack promised never to break the rules again, he realized that his father was right. He just wanted to take care of him, and he loved him very much.

Finally, much later, when he was able to play on the skateboard again, he was at least 50 meters away from the hill, and when he was going to get close to

that area, he would get off, pick up the skateboard, and walk away, then climb back on.

When he wanted to play on wider terrain, he would go with his father to a park where he could more safely practice other tricks.

Parents make rules that may seem annoying to you, but they only do it to take care of you and protect you. Don't break them, because something bad can happen to you.

Samuel and the Lesson of Imperfection

How does it make you feel when you make mistakes? Do you feel bad? Do you say mean things to yourself? Mistakes come in all shapes and forms, and you have to know that they are amazing, even if it surprises

you to know it. You can learn from them. Mistakes are the path to success and improvement.

Samuel woke up before his alarm went off. He felt happy and excited about the day ahead of him. He had a routine every morning to get his things done before leaving for school.

When the alarm went off, Samuel settled himself to start getting ready for school. He turned off the alarm, and the morning silence reigned throughout the house.

He stretched every muscle in his body and slowly got out of bed.

He felt a push of adrenaline to get out of bed. It was the best way to start the day.

He made his bed just as his mother had instructed. He went to school that day and felt that everything had gone just as he had timed it with exact minutes so that nothing would go wrong. He was very methodical.

Mistakes didn't go well for him; he felt he couldn't, and that's why he was so exact with his things.

When class was over, he would pack up his things and leave everything very organized to go home.

His friend Victor appeared next to him and told him something about the game on Friday—that they would have to arrive a little earlier.

"No way," Samuel said. He already had everything planned. He would have to check again, so he opened his bag and started scribbling that Friday's time was changing at practice.

The bell rang for the second time, announcing that everyone had to leave now, and for Samuel, it was a sign that he had to go. So, he got ready and ran out as soon as he had finished planning the message Victor had given him.

When he left, he went straight home; he had the minutes counted to arrive on time and do his things without missing anything.

Having Victor make him rewrite things in the diary he had already saved didn't sit well with him. It was wasting valuable minutes. He would have to manage that better in the future.

Once at home, he began to take everything out of his suitcase, arranging it with millimetric care, but soon

he began to worry because something happened that altered, or rather, ruined the day in a catastrophic way for him.

A math notebook was missing, in which he had written down the homework he had to do and hand in the following day.

"I can't have left that notebook behind," he said.

He had never left a notebook behind, and as he took things out of his bag again and again, hoping to find it, he felt deep down that he would not see it again that day.

He thought of Victor, thinking that by interrupting him, he had made him forget that notebook. If he had at least waited for him to finish putting it away, it wouldn't have stayed with him. He felt anger and frustration and clenched his fists. He couldn't believe he had made such a serious mistake.

He told himself that he would never have forgotten the notebook if he hadn't been interrupted.

This incident had put him in a very bad mood. He went into the room and slammed it shut.

"Who is that walking around the house like a giant and knocking down doors?" said his father, who appeared in his room.

He was upset, so he was not afraid to show what he felt and let his father know.

"I'm really mad at Victor for leaving my math notebook on my seat, and now I won't be able to turn in an assignment tomorrow."

The father looked at him with a hint of sadness and, at the same time, with a smile.

"What a problem."

"Yes," said Samuel, "now I don't know what I'm going to do; tomorrow's whole day is ruined for me."

"He distracted me at the end of the class to tell me that they had changed the training time on Friday, and that's why he stayed with me because I was putting things in my backpack."

His father was someone who was in a good mood, so he knew that what his son was feeling, while he had a right to be angry, was misplaced.

"Son, that sounds to me like you're the one who made a mistake."

Samuel looked at his father with annoyance; he couldn't believe what he had just said.

"What?" he said.

"I think Victor was helping you. He warned you about a last-minute change, and you made the mistake of leaving the notebook. How would you have known about the change if he didn't tell you? Besides, he had no idea that you had everything timed at that moment when you put things away."

Samuel realized that his father was right, but instead of feeling relief, he now felt more anger.

"Mistake?" he said.

"Yes."

"Did I make a mistake?"

"Yes."

He could not credit that he had made a mistake, for he could not remember when he had last done so.

As he analyzed all this, he began to worry more. He saw his father, and his features softened, more so when he noticed that he was looking at him with love. His father reached over, put a hand on his shoulder, and stroked his head.

"Why are you so angry, son?"

He answered with a cry, hugged him to unburden himself, and tried to speak, stammering.

"I made a mistake!" he said with an effort.

His father let him unburden himself, and when he stopped crying, he hugged him and began to talk to him with much love: "Son, it's okay to make mistakes because they are a good thing; you don't have to fear that because they give you the opportunity to think creatively, solve problems, and learn new things about yourself."

Samuel did not say anything, but he was no longer crying. He wiped his tears.

"What does that mean?"

"You're a wonderful boy, a very good student, and responsible, but you put a lot of pressure on yourself to be perfect as if you were a watch, and you don't

have to be like that. Perfect is not good. It doesn't exist. You want to keep everything neat and tidy in a way that overwhelms you. Look at your younger brother, who has everything messy and doesn't have a pair of matching socks together."

Samuel laughed, thinking about that. He couldn't bear to see how his brother could live like that.

"The fact that your brother is like that doesn't make him bad because he's doing well in school. Imperfect is not bad."

He thought of his younger brother, who, yes, was messy, but he wasn't bad. Always kind and good at things, with talents.

"Perfection doesn't mean that your life will be stress-free, but when you keep trying to be perfect, you miss moments where you can learn more about who you are and how you handle change; mistakes are great."

Samuel cried again at the thought of the mistake, but he was beginning to understand what his father wanted to tell him.

They gave each other a big hug, and he told him that he was thinking about how he could find a solution to the mistake.

"I forgot the notebook, but now that I think about it, I know what the teacher wants. I will be able to do it in another notebook or on a few sheets of paper, and then at home, I will put everything in the notebook."

"You see, there is a solution, and there was no need to react that way. You see, it was easy, and if you hadn't forgotten that notebook, you wouldn't have had to think to find the solution. How do you feel?"

"Great."

Samuel started to do his homework and completed it in a while. That night in his bed, he wondered what it would be like if the next day, when he made his bed, he wasn't so radical in making it up or even leaving it unmade for a day.

When he woke up the next day, he made the bed; it wasn't perfect, but he didn't care!

Samuel knew that even if he made mistakes, he didn't have to be frustrated like that, but that he could take advantage of it and grow to be successful. He was already happy with that. He saw it as a learning experience.

Learn from mistakes and adversity; when you do, you can grow in many ways, and you will become more amazing than you already are. Every mistake is a lesson; don't forget that.

The Guardian Tree Adventure

Have you ever seen danger when no one else has? Have you come across places that could hurt you and tell others? Are you trustworthy? This is an adventure story where being observant and warning are part of teamwork.

Peter loved the vacations—times when he didn't have to take notebooks, beyond the review he did with his mom for a while each day—but there was no homework, uniforms, or getting up early. It was the best time of the year after Christmas.

After lunch, a group of boys would get together to look for adventures. Since they lived in an area that had a rural setting, they could wander among the trees, cliffs, and small mountains they explored and see the birds, squirrels, and some wild animals grazing.

Peter enjoyed going with them because each one had a talent; for example, Max was good at climbing trees. Paul was an expert at jumping over rocks, and Luke had a keen ear for hearing movements in the bushes and warning of danger.

"Let's go," said Max when Peter opened the door to his house.

"I'll throw the water in the backpack, and we'll go," said Peter cheerfully.

Paul and Max greeted him by raising their hands.

This day's excursion was important. They would climb a little higher than normal to a tree that

everyone called Jobo. It was gigantic. His mother said it was older than his grandfather. It was a fat tree, almost as wide as a car and as tall as a four-story house, with wide branches, full of many leaves and seeds as if it had pimples. It was a very old tree that had silently watched the city grow.

The plan was to go climbing. Max had a plan to climb it and see the city. According to him, his brother had told him that from the top, you could see the whole city in its fullness, and he didn't want to miss that view. Although his plan was for everyone to climb, including Peter, Peter was afraid of heights and was looking for a way out so as not to go up.

The group of friends left Peter's house and made their way up the mountain. As soon as they left the small town, they had to cross a bridge, but the adventure was calling, and since it was summertime, the river that ran under it was low, barely a stream, and they all passed by betting on who would get to the other side first, over the stones, choosing the ones that were dry so as not to slip.

Although they were not exempt from injuries, sometimes they stumbled and scraped, but they shook it off, rubbed themselves a little, and continued the adventure.

Peter noticed that Max was having more fun that day than ever. He looked excited.

"When I get to that old tree, I will climb it like I climb the stairs in my house to go to the second floor."

"I'll climb it when I get to my apartment with an elevator." Paul said.

"Yes, because the Jobo has an elevator." Luke said.

They all laughed.

"What I mean is that I will climb it faster than all of you. Let's see, Peter, how are you going to climb it?"

Peter, who said the last thing he wanted to do was climb, said with a smile,

"I'll climb it in one jump."

"Oh, he's worse," said Max. Now he's jumping like a spring.

They all laughed and continued betting on who would climb it first.

As they climbed up the mountain, the tree that could be seen from the city here began to grow taller and

taller, as if it were a giant guarding the whole area and sleeping, hoping not to be disturbed.

There was a moment where they all remained silent; the slope was steep, and also, that tree seemed to create a shadow over the entire lack of mountains. Although none of them recognized it, they felt a little afraid for the adventure they had prepared.

Besides, Max had said that the last one to arrive or the first one to chicken out was a rotten egg. None of them wanted to be.

"It looks like it's bigger than we were told," said Peter.

"Yes, it's going to be our big challenge," said Max.

"Challenge for you. You'll climb it like a turtle," said Paul.

"Challenge for you, who will see me from below with regret for not having reached the top." said Luke.

Each one of them thought that he would get there first. Well, all of them except Peter, who, while he was climbing and breathing through his mouth because of the great effort it represented to climb, thought about how to save himself from not climbing that

tree, and every step made him look up more and more to contemplate the height.

Finally, the mountain stopped climbing, and they reached a plain with a shadow that made it look like dusk, but in reality, it was the branches of the Jobo tree, so wide and abundant that they covered the sun. The tree was fatter than their parents told them; it was at least two cars wide and tall. They could not calculate it. It looked like a building.

The first branch was several meters high.

"Wow, it will be quite a challenge," said Max when he saw it up close. He slapped his hands as if to warm them up and approached.

Paul took out some matted gloves he had to play with, which he said would help him not to get hurt. Luke spat on his hands to get a better grip, although he immediately felt disgusted.

"It's now, then," said Paul, who started to climb but began to slip. It was hard for him to do it.

"I'll get there first," said Luke, who jumped up and grabbed a bump. He pushed himself up, but he wasn't strong enough.

"This is mine," said Max, who concentrated and began to climb.

With each movement, he fell into a bump or hole in the tree, and soon after, he was a few meters off the ground. The others watched him from below, frightened and excited.

He reached the first branch.

"Everyone is a rotten egg," he shouted from above, excited.

He continued climbing, the others silently watching as he seemed to shrink as he climbed.

Peter noticed something strange on one of the branches and shouted:

"Beware! That branch is rotten. You're going to fall."

"It's nothing. It's nothing."

He continued climbing, and the branch creaked and broke. It was all a matter of a thousandth of a second. Max fell a couple of meters, but in a reflex, he grabbed another branch and looked very scared. He almost fell.

This scare was enough for him to descend. When he reached the bottom, he said,

"I was going to reach the top, but as none of you dared, I am the winner."

They were all so overwhelmed by the branch that no one took credit away from him.

They walked home down the mountain in silence.

On the way back, at one point, Max came over and put his hand on Peter's shoulder and smiled at him as if to say "Thank you" for warning him. Peter felt that he had given him the understanding that he was someone to trust and was attentive to the team.

After this incident, the next few adventures they took were less risky. The lesson helped them realize that they were humans and could get hurt if they were not responsible in their games.

Peter continued to enjoy the vacations with his friends, going out to different places; they went fishing; they climbed, but not very high; and from that day on, they saw the Jobo with respect. It was a tree that did not like to be disturbed.

Being part of a team implies being aware of what may happen, warning in time to help others, and sometimes reserving to take some risks, even when others want to do it.

Listen to that inner voice that tells you not to do it, and when you are in a group, warn others of what may be in the near future.

The Neighbor's Helping Hand

Have you seen that there are people who need help? Have you discovered how much you can do for someone with a little effort on your part? The best way to help someone else is to surprise them by being kind, so you show them you care and make a difference. That's what this story is all about.

Michael was working on a puzzle about a powerful superhero. He was looking through all the colorful

pieces to find the one that went in that space. He was a little frustrated, but at the same time, he was enjoying putting the sections together.

He heard something outside and looked out the window. It was Mrs. Emily who was on her way home, someone too old to walk with great effort with a cane. She had something on her leg, and this made it difficult for her to walk. Later, he would know that it was a splint; apparently, she had had an accident.

He put down the puzzle and decided to go find out what was going on.

"Dad"

"Tell me, son."

"Mrs. Emily walks with a cane and has something on her leg."

"That's too bad. Let's go see her; maybe she needs our help."

Michael liked the idea of going to see what was wrong with the lady. He liked how his father liked to help others and was kind. He shook his hand, and they walked outside in the direction of the lady's house.

They knocked on the door, and the lady opened it a couple of minutes later.

"Hello, John." She said, "How can I help you?"

"My son saw you arrive just now. We came to see how you were doing."

"Oh, how nice of you. Please come in."

The woman sat down. Her leg was hurting.

"What happened to her?" Michael asked.

"I was going out to buy fruit for the week, and I slipped on the corner, my foot bent. It didn't break, but they put this on it so it would heal. I have a crack. Thank goodness it didn't break because, at this age, the bones don't weld the same."

Michael didn't think it was lucky at all; he thought it was a bad thing. He agreed that at least the lady hadn't had a broken bone.

"That's too bad."

"Not so bad; in a few weeks, you'll see me bouncing and happy. I'll be good again."

"How are you going to do your things?" His father asked.

"I think I'll ask the boy on the corner to come and help me, the errand boy. I'll have to pay him, but no way."

They visited her for a while longer and then went home. That night, while they were all at the dinner table, Michael talked about Mrs. Emily and asked about her family, wondering if she didn't have anyone to come and take care of her children or siblings. His father told him that she was single, never married, and now alone in the world.

"I wish I could help her," Michael said.

"What a good heart you have," said his father.

The subject remained there, but late at night, while he was with his father solving the superhero puzzle, Michael said to him as he placed a piece, I know how we can help the lady.

"I know how we can help Mrs. Emily. We can do some things to her house so that she doesn't go from one place to another."

"How do you do it?"

"Surely the doctor asked her not to walk so much, so we can help her with house chores so she can rest and be calm."

"I like the idea."

They both spent a long time thinking about what they could do to help the lady, going to check things at home and cleaning, and they agreed that they would bring her food. The mom said that now she would make the meals for one more plate, and so they would bring her every meal.

"Today, when we were there, I realized that there were several things to do." said the father.

"I saw the house a little dirty; I could sweep and mop."

"Yes, there must be something to do, and we can help."

Michael's father felt very proud of his son for what he had proposed; he realized that he had inherited his good heart. They agreed that the next day he would propose to Mrs. Emily the help they were going to offer her.

Before closing the bedroom door to go to sleep, he said to him,

"I feel very proud of you and of your desire to help others. I congratulate you, son."

Michael felt good and went to sleep with a very gratifying feeling in his chest.

The next day, they went and proposed to Mrs. Emily to help, and after she said no because she felt sorry to bother them, she agreed, recognizing that she could use a hand. The father began to check the house, change some light bulbs, and fix some wires that were about to short out. In the bathroom, he fixed some dripping faucets, checked a clogged pipe, and fixed a humidity that had a white stain on a wall.

Michael cleaned the house thoroughly, dusted the dust, fed and pampered a Siamese cat she had, combed it, and removed all the dead hairs.

He cleaned the gutters that had a lot of leaves and were causing internal leakage when it rained.

Mrs. Emily apparently felt at ease with the presence because she went to take a nap, and father and son laughed when the lady snored and seemed to be at ease. Since they were both free, they decided to play hide and seek for a while. They had a lot of fun.

After checking everything inside, including eating at Mrs. Emily's table, when Michael's mother brought the food, they went out to check the plants in the yard, to prune the lawn a little, and to cut some branches of an old tree that threatened to crush the roof of the house.

Michael would never forget the look on Mrs. Emily's face when she woke up and saw her house. With all the repairs done and the outside clean, with the lawn flushed and the plants cared for, she was impressed with how young, strong hands had accomplished so much. Michael and his dad were tired from the day's work but happy.

"Thank you; it's been a long time since I've seen my house as beautiful as it is today. Everything is beautiful. Thank you, thank you."

"It's an honor, we want it to get better soon, said Michael."

"Thank you for your help, young man."

The lady wiped her tears. She was moved, and she felt loved and supported.

Michael could not stand it and hugged his neighbor, giving her a kiss on the cheek.

"We just wanted to help you feel better."

"I feel much better, even my leg hurts less. Thank you."

The next few days, the support was visits, some small chores, and lunch every hour.

Then Mrs. Emily said that she could cook for herself and that she had improved a lot.

For about a week, they didn't hear from her. One day, there was a knock at the door. Michael opened the door and saw Mrs. Emily without crutches, and she looked younger than before, refreshed. She had something in her hands. It was a chocolate cake.

"Thank you!" Michael said to her.

"Thank you for the help. You have given me these days. More than feeling sick, I felt sad and lonely because I had to do everything by myself."

Mrs. Emily looked very happy and grateful, with a deep affection and thankfulness that came from the bottom of her heart. The three of them ate cake and tasted coffee and tea.

No matter how old you are or what you do, a simple gesture can brighten someone else's life. You can't imagine the needs that others have. Don't be afraid to help.

Every idea you have put into action, just like Michael proposed to help the neighbor and made her convalescence more bearable, can help others. You have a special gift in this world, and only you can share it. It is time. Be kind and help others feel amazing, and you will feel amazing yourself.

The Persistent Dreamer

Have you ever started chasing dreams only to feel like they're too far away? Do you want to achieve something, but it doesn't work out the first time? You may not know it, but in order to achieve dreams, you have to work hard to achieve them. Patience is important and is the cornerstone.

Leo had a dream since he was a child, and it was to be a famous writer, where people would read the stories that flowed in his mind and transported him through unimaginable worlds. Since he was a little boy, he created stories and learned to read at a very young age. He devoured every book that came into his hands in a short time.

He had written some short stories and poems for his pets, his parents, and his grandfather. What he loved most was his collection of short stories, which together made a great story.

Every day, when he looked at his writings, he felt very happy. He was inspired and came up with new stories.

One day, he wanted to participate in a joint reading with great writers from the city. He wanted to be an inspiration for other children.

He asked his mother if he could participate and if she would buy him more notebooks and pencils.

His mother told him that as soon as she left, she would go to the stationery store to get everything he had asked for.

His mother showed up with a ream of paper, several notebooks, and many colored pencils. That day was one of the happiest. He went to his room and set up a small studio, where he spent hours writing and thinking up stories. Although now that he had set up this studio, he was not so happy with his work. Deep down, he believed he could write it better: change verbs, eliminate adjectives, add more poetry to some sentences, and change outcomes.

He asked himself many questions about how to make his work better.

If I want to be a famous writer, I have to learn how to be one.

He found a creative writing class at the local library and signed up to improve his writing. He saw that he was making many mistakes and worked to improve them. Over the next few days, he felt that his writing was getting better and better.

When he felt confident enough, he went to a literary café where the most famous writers in the city were present and wanted to apply to do a reading for everyone.

The woman who was attending smiled sweetly when she saw him,

"Thank you for visiting us, but sadly, we are not accepting new writers now. Maybe you can come next year because we already have a full schedule."

Leo felt very sad, but this did nothing but push him to keep preparing. He went to more classes and worked. He even got more praise for his writing, and those who read it were overwhelmed by his solid stories and unforgettable characters.

The following year, he went with another collection of writings for them to see. The woman who had served him last year was still there, and upon seeing him, she was surprised. She noticed that he had improvements in his writing, but sadly, she turned him down with almost the exact same words.

Leo could not believe it.

"Don't you like my writing? " He asked.

The woman came clean.

"Your work is excellent, but you can improve more. You just need to keep practicing. I'm not going to accept what you're proposing this time."

Leo went home disappointed, sat down in the living room, and looked at all the books he had been accumulating for years. He had been working on becoming a better writer for some time. He remembered each of the classes he had taken and remembered a pattern in everything:

Each of the writers there had been writing for years before they were recognized. As he read biographies of writers, he realized that many of them were rejected and had a hard time getting the place they had now.

Leo smiled a calmer smile and went back to writing. He continued to study and began to create a collection, a sort of little saga that flowed from his soul, the words flowing with a beauty he had never felt before.

When he was about to finish this work that he had decided to write on the computer, he inadvertently deleted one of the chapters, the one he considered to be one of the important ones.

"It can't be!" He said it regretfully.

He tried by all means to recover the file; he even went to a programmer, but he was told that there was

nothing to be done. He had left work with a gap—the plot part, not the poetic or philosophical part that he had worked on in others.

Leo sat down to cry, heartbroken by what had happened. He had worked so hard on creating these works, and now, in such a foolish way, he had lost one of the best chapters.

Venting, he went back to the computer and rearranged things. The next day, he sat down and reviewed each of the chapters, even the one he had missed, and discovered that he had achieved something abstract, that this missing chapter could leave scenes open to interpretation, and that they themselves represented an interesting proposition.

When it was time to go to the famous literary café to knock on the door again, he did not feel so sure. He did not feel so sure because he expected the woman's rejection.

"It's good to see you again," said the woman when she saw him enter. "I hope you surprise me this year as always."

"This year, I didn't want to bring loose writings or snippets of stories, but I was encouraged to bring a composition that was accidentally interesting."

"Well, let's read it, then."

Leo showed her the whole text, and the woman asked for time to read it calmly. He didn't want to leave but stayed browsing through the books. The woman went through the stories, finding interesting plots with twists she did not expect, philosophical phrases throughout the writing that she liked, reflective themes, and poetry in many lines. No doubt, it was the product of someone who had put effort into creating it.

"I feel something is missing here," the woman, an expert reader, told him.

Leo, with some embarrassment, told her what had happened.

"Well, although the gap is felt, I noticed it because I've read other things of yours, but a zero reader hasn't, and I love this because each reader can draw their own interpretation. I'll be glad to have you here, reading with the other writers this year."

Leo felt like he was going to lose his heart from all the jumping he was doing, but he had made it. He and his parents celebrated with a dinner out, and he excitedly awaited the day when all the writers and people who came to the café to see writers would come to hear his readings and start rubbing elbows with other writers.

"We are very proud of you," said his parents.

"Are you proud because I wrote something good?"

"Yes, but more so because you didn't give up despite rejections. You always stood up. You could have given up at any time, even with trouble on the way, but you showed love and patience, and now you have the prize for the effort."

He went home happy that day and would soon enjoy a full house reading with people in awe of a young man with such writing gifts.

Leo was in awe the day he saw everyone's impression as he brought his reading to a close. He was almost in tears as he watched everyone rise to their feet and give him a standing ovation. Usually, they did it out of formality or from their seats, but now they seemed truly immersed and moved by his story.

You should never give up on your dreams, even if many obstacles appear along the way. Leo didn't. He knew that it takes time to achieve your dreams.

It may take longer than expected to achieve your dreams, but you can get what you want, so don't be discouraged by the obstacles you encounter along the way. Keep building your craft, and soon you will be the best writer, painter, or whatever you want to be.

The Roller Skates Dilemma

What do you think about honesty? Have you ever had the chance to keep something and return it? In this story, you'll get to know about a boy who desired a pair of roller skates with all his heart.

Daniel didn't want to go, but his mother told him he couldn't stay alone at home. His father wouldn't be

back until the evening, so they had to go to the supermarket because they had nothing in the pantry. While they were in the store, in an area next to the technology section, he found something that immediately caught his attention. It was the sports section, and on one of the shelves were some incredible roller skates—beautiful, unlike any he had ever seen. The wheels lit up. They were as black as the night and had rainbow-colored laces.

From that day on, all he could think about were the roller skates. It was love at first sight.

Daniel was so passionate about those roller skates that he made drawings of himself wearing them, skating on many avenues and streets. Then, every day after leaving school, he went with his mother to do something in the area, and from where he was, he saw the roller skates in the display case.

"I want those roller skates, Mom," he said to his mother.

To which his mother replied,

"Yes, they're nice; I'm glad you like them."

One day, they went with his younger brother, and he said,

"But you have good roller skates at home, and you never wear them."

"Those roller skates are all worn out, and one-wheel wobbles," Daniel said.

"But they still work," his brother said.

Daniel didn't say anything but gave his brother a dirty look.

"I want those roller skates that Mom thinks I don't need, and my silly brother says I don't need them because I already have some."

A week passed, and the roller skates he always saw in that display case were no longer there; they had been replaced by a soccer ball.

"Where are my roller skates?" Daniel said, a little anxious.

"At home, in the storeroom where you left them," his brother said.

"Not those, shush!" Instead, Daniel said, "those from the store."

"They probably sold them," his mother said.

"I wanted them."

"I'm sorry, these things happen."

Now he felt very sad, thinking he would never be happy.

A few days later, as Daniel was returning home, he saw an identical pair of roller skates to the ones in the store at the park.

"Whose roller skates are these?" Daniel asked as if claiming something that belonged to him.

But no one was nearby, and he saw another skate next to it; they were a pair. So Daniel thought that the roller skates were there for him, waiting. He couldn't leave them there, so he took them and went home triumphantly.

Upon entering, he hid them in the storeroom, where they couldn't be found. Then he said he would leave them there until he spoke to his parents. Then, every day, when he had the opportunity, he went to see the beautiful roller skates.

Later, he believed that having those roller skates there caused pressure in his stomach. He thought about them, and it wasn't good.

Days later, while at school, he accidentally overheard a conversation between two boys.

"Did you hear what happened to Larry?"

"No, what?"

"He lost his new roller skates. He left them in the park near his house, and they weren't there when he returned."

"I can't believe it; I always told him not to leave them around; they were so cool, and someone could steal them."

"Yeah, poor guy, they were a birthday present. When he came back, there was nothing there."

"I would never leave such cool roller skates alone. He didn't deserve this. He must be devastated."

After school, several kids went to the park to help Larry look for the roller skates, but they didn't find anything. Larry was very upset because his father even worked extra hours to gather the money and give him the roller skates for his birthday, and they hadn't lasted long because of his irresponsibility.

Daniel spent that day feeling down, thinking about what had happened to Larry and that he had the roller skates that didn't belong to him.

After leaving class, he went to his room and had a stomach ache and an unpleasant emptiness that made him feel like sleeping.

He thought about how he could fix this problem he had gotten himself into.

"I didn't hear you," his mother said behind him, and Daniel jumped in fright.

"Are you okay? Why are you like this, with your eyes shining like you have cried?"

His mother took the drawing and looked at it closely.

"Are you still sad about those roller skates we didn't buy you?"

"Kind of, but it's not what you think."

Daniel sighed and told her everything. When he finished, his mother said,

"You must return those roller skates to that boy; he must be very sad."

"Yes, I have to return the roller skates."

His mother hugged Daniel tightly and kissed his forehead.

"You're doing the right thing."

"I know where Larry lives. I know his mom, so it's time to return those roller skates."

When they arrived at the house, Daniel told them how he had found the roller skates at the park and picked them up.

Larry's father smiled with great joy and said,

"Thank you; we were hoping they would turn up because Larry was very sad about them. Thank you for returning them."

On the way back home, Daniel smiled, feeling good about himself despite what had happened. He was grateful. His stomach, which had tormented him those days, was now fine. Now he felt happy because he had done a good deed.

He felt very proud of himself because he had done what was right. His mother also looked proud, driving

in silence, but the smile on her face showed that she was proud of her son.

Never keep something that isn't yours, even if you desire it greatly. If you know to whom something you found belongs, you return it.

The Price of Integrity

Have you ever had the opportunity to cheat? Have you done it? Do you think it's okay to do so? This story is about how an opportunity may not be the best if your conscience has a price.

Luke doesn't consider himself the bravest person in the world. For example, if he has to face a snake, he'd

rather run away and do it well because snakes are to be avoided. He has never fought a lion, nor does he even pet other people's dogs. But he has faced terrifying things, like standing up to the boys on his soccer team when necessary. He did it like a very mature boy, pridefully filling his parents and relatives.

During the soccer season in which Luke's team participated, they debated many matches. They qualified until they reached the semifinals and the beloved final to obtain victory. They prepared for an entire year for that great season.

During the previous season, Luke's team, the Reds, came from behind in an incredible playoff final. The entire crowd stood up and cheered, full of energy. It was one of the best games in the history of that field.

Luke and his team lost more games than they had won as the season progressed, and they were ranked sixth out of eight in the standings.

In the end, they had to face a white team that was strong and third in the rankings. They were afraid because they had strong kicks and were sure to win. They wanted to play in the final round, just like the Reds.

They scored the first goal and didn't let the Whites catch up. They had this plan to go on the offensive, with the forwards as the most aggressive, and not to let the whites into their area of the field; the plan was the offense. This was working very well, and the Reds outscored the white team by two goals and thus qualified for the next round.

The following weekend was the semifinal. They would face the Yellow Team. Luke had very thick and defined legs. His kicks were strong and deadly. On the yellow team, the player in the same position as Luke also had thick and strong legs to kick and a lot of agility to take the ball away. He always managed to take the ball away and come on the offensive.

Luke saw a boy like him advancing with great force and being as tall as his father. He was several heads taller. His steps were fast, and keeping up with him was difficult. Luke advanced with great force but couldn't prevent him from making a shot; it would have been a goal if it weren't for the goalkeeper.

Luke stood there, with his foot ready but without the ball, as if responding to a ballet movement. He couldn't do anything; he had already lost the ball.

Everything became more complicated as none of the boys on Luke's team could do anything; apparently, the Yellows had studied their strategies and were attacking with all their might. It seemed like the ground had turned into a slippery surface. The Reds lost by three goals. But it wasn't over yet; they had to play another game to secure third place and take home a trophy.

The following week, Luke and the other boys on the team arrived at the field earlier. That day, they would play against a team where they knew many players, boys who had been on the team in other seasons, and even a coach they had met years before. They were all silent on the field, and their breaths were the only sounds that could be heard. They went onto the field and prepared everything for the game. The moment the referee blew the whistle, it came faster than they expected.

The opposing team ran with the ball and tried to score with force. The score numbers started to jump because the first goal was scored. Everyone jumped, and Luke realized they were beginning to lose, which he regretted. Although they felt that on that day, with the lucky uniform they wore, they were not lucky enough to win. They were falling behind by one goal,

and there was very little time left to score and tie the game, to go to penalties, or to win. There was an opportunity to do it. The ball was out of bounds.

"The Reds have the turn to throw the ball," said the referee.

It turned out that the referee had not noticed which team had the turn to do so. When the player threw the ball, he took it in his hands to make the throw. Luke noticed, but the referee did not, who had touched the ball last. That defined who had the right to throw the ball and try to win. Luke and the others on the red team wanted to win. If the Whites took the ball, they would get to the goal and win by a goal. On the other hand, if Luke had stayed quiet, the Reds would have had a chance to keep playing and win.

"Thank you," said the referee when he heard Luke's confession. He took the ball from the Reds and passed it to the other team. Some complained about what was happening. Some seemed to be on the verge of tears from what they saw. Although they came close, Luke's team lost by three points, but the boys ended up with beautiful medals in fourth place and ribbons that said they had been the best at that moment. Everyone thought it was great. Luke's old coach approached him before he left.

"Luke, I saw what you did there," he said, pointing to the court with his finger. "What you did makes me very proud of you, and I'm not talking about the game, do you know what I mean?"

Then they asked Luke if he felt scared when he thought about telling the truth to the referee and how this would cost them the third-place victory. If he thought about the reprisals, they would come later. But when he heard this, he confessed,

"Well, honestly, it wasn't quite like you're telling me. They were angry with me, but I was sure they wouldn't hate me. But if I didn't say anything, I knew I would be the one angry with myself, so I chose to feel good despite the consequences."

Always tell the truth and don't cheat, no matter the consequences. There's nothing as good as having a clear conscience.

The Bonding Mural

Are there objects in your family that seem ancient to you and tell you stories of relatives you never knew? Do you take care of those pieces as if they were the most valuable treasure in the world? What would happen if something were to end up with that object? If you use your imagination, surely, despite the circumstances, you can make new family memories about each other's pieces.

Luke was looking at the vase next to the fireplace in the house. He was lying on a sofa in one of those moments when you don't want to do anything. Bored, he began to contemplate each place, and his eyes fell on the piece that seemed to have been in the house all his life because, apparently, his grandfather's father brought it when he escaped from who knows what country because of a war situation that he doesn't remember how it happened. Everyone wanted the vase because, apparently, it was the only thing great-grandfather had brought with him.

Luke saw his two brothers, who were just a few meters away from him. The younger one was fighting with the other one about something in the car game they had. It had something to do with some buildings, and the street they had entered was in the opposite direction.

Their tempers were getting hotter, and they were fighting more intensely. Their mother would peek through the door and authoritatively ask them to calm down, or they would go to bed.

Although their mother appeared from time to time to bring order, it seemed that the two of them were getting cranky as the minutes went by.

"Thomas and Johnny, if they keep up that fight, they're really going to go to sleep."

"I'm sorry, mom," said Thomas, who was the oldest, "but Johnny doesn't want to listen; you can't go through here."

"Let him go; don't worry about it, don't forget that they are playing."

Thomas raised his eyes to the sky. Luke rolled his eyes. He couldn't stand those fights. He took the cell phone and started to see things—a way to get away from the fight between the two of them.

Somewhere in his brain, he heard that the kids seemed to be fighting more; things moved, and soon there was a loud crash where the world seemed to stop.

Luke looked away from the phone and saw the direction of his brothers, who looked frozen. They didn't move a muscle, and a terrified grimace was directed at their brother as if asking, "Did we do it?" Surely Luke's now look also confirmed to them that they had indeed made a grave mistake. They had broken the vase with so much affection.

"What did they do?" Luke said it almost in a whisper.

"It was an accident."

"Dad is going to be furious."

His siblings, who, a second before, had been fighting for a long time, now trembled and looked in the direction of the door where their parents would surely appear at any moment since the cracking sound when the vase broke had been loud.

Luke put down the phone and went to look at the pieces; almost everything had been destroyed, except for a piece that was in the center of the ornament, egg-shaped and dark blue.

"Can you explain to me what is going on here?" It was the mother who had appeared in the doorway and seemed to be processing everything her eyes were seeing.

"It was an accident, Mom."

She didn't have time to answer, as the father appeared in the doorway as well.

"What was it that creaked? What broke?" The father was silent for a moment and then added, "The vase!" "Who did it?"

The two brothers looked at each other, and Thomas spoke.

"It was us. We were playing, and..."

"Don't say any more," said the father.

He approached Luke. He had a strange expression. He took him by the arm firmly, but without squeezing him, he took him to the door and told him, "Please, take your brothers to the room and stay there for a while. We have to clean this well and avoid leaving pieces on the floor to hurt the soles of our feet."

Luke nodded and motioned to his siblings, who seemed relieved to get out of there.

"Is Dad going to punish us?" Thomas asked his brother.

"I don't think so; he would have done it already. But he asked us to stay here."

"We didn't mean to," said John.

"I know they were playing. It was an accident."

John had a little runny nose. Luke thought he would have to entertain them and make sure they didn't do anything wrong.

"Shall we play a game?" he suggested.

"I don't want to," said John. Dad will come to scold us right now.

"Yes, sure," said Thomas, who seemed to be thinking about the consequences too.

"We should have thought about what we could break," said John.

"And I should have at least given them a look and not neglected them and let them end up like that."

"Don't feel bad," said Luke. "I think we can do something to make up for what happened. Do you think we can try to create something?"

"What do you have in mind?" said Thomas.

"I'll do anything."

"I think they'll like the idea."

Luke thought about how the vase was already ruined, except for the piece he was holding; the rest was safely in the trash by now. But something could be done to create new memories so that later this day would be the beginning of a new chapter in the family history.

"We can take the poster board—that nice one we have but never use at school—and create a nice mural with each of us on it."

"What is that?" Thomas asked.

"Art like those we see in the streets that people make with spray paint; remember the other day you saw one of a cat?"

"Ah! I like it. Shall we make a cat?"

"Well, it's not what I thought, but something like that for mom and dad to get that gesture from us."

The two brothers got excited, and their heads started flying with ideas. Thomas took out the cardboard, John looked for the pot with brushes and colors, and Luke took out the tempera paints and acrylics. In a couple of minutes, they had a whole workshop set up to start making art.

The first thing Luke did was to take the piece that had been left over from the vase; he took the school glue and smeared it all over the back, then he placed the piece on the middle of the cardboard and left it there very still until it would stick.

The two brothers began to paint. They decided to make a family story with the two of them playing with one's hand on the other's shoulder, showing that they were a family that loved each other no matter what. At the top, Luke made the back silhouette of their mom and dad, hugging, who seemed to be contemplating them. From the center of the piece of vase, he made some white streaks that seemed to be a light coming out of it and covering everyone, as if showing that despite the circumstances, that memory would always be present.

"What are they doing?" asked the mother, who appeared in the room.

The siblings looked at each other with frightened faces; Luke was the one who answered.

"We are making a new family mural."

"Oh, but that's beautiful what you've done!"

"Will you help us?" John said in a sweet voice.

"Of course, I will." Mom said this and sat down with everyone.

Soon, Dad appeared and saw what was going on. It didn't take him long to understand the meaning, and

he sat down with everyone. Each one contributed ideas, and they reinforced the play.

Two days later, without saying anything to anyone, Dad took the work they had done and, in the afternoon, returned with it in a very nice frame. Now, on the fireplace rested that painting made from love, which started from an accident.

Accidents happen; they are part of life, and we cannot always escape them. The family had known how to take advantage of the children's idea of creating a new object out of something that symbolized a family moment.

If we make mistakes or something breaks, it is normal to feel sad about it, but it is not a bad thing to die for because you can take advantage of it and, from the pieces, create a new opportunity that can be even more beautiful than it was before. Besides, it is an opportunity to strengthen ties.

Made in the USA
Las Vegas, NV
25 November 2023

81479733R00056